© 2010 Disney Enterprises, Inc.
Published by Hachette Partworks Ltd
ISBN: 978-1-906965-32-7
Date of Printing: March 2010
Printed in Singapore by Tien Wah Press

One evening, a girl called Tiana was sitting in the New Orleans mansion of her friend Charlotte. Together they were listening to Tiana's mother, Eudora, tell them a story about a prince who had been turned into a frog.

"There is no way in this whole wide world I would ever, ever, *ever* – I mean never – kiss a frog! Yuck!" Tiana insisted.

"I would kiss a *hundred* frogs if I could marry a prince and be a princess!" Charlotte exclaimed.

At bedtime that night, Tiana's parents encouraged her to wish on the Evening Star. Tiana and her father, James, dreamed of opening a restaurant some day at the old sugar mill down by the river. So that would be her wish.

James gently reminded his daughter that she could help her dream come true with some hard work. Then, looking at his family, he said, "Just never lose sight of what's really important."

Years went by and
Tiana's father died –
but she held on to their
dream. To save money
for her restaurant, she
worked very hard as
a waitress. She rarely
had time for fun.

One day, a glamorous visitor arrived in New Orleans – handsome Prince Naveen of Maldonia. Naveen didn't seem like a typical prince – he liked to play jazz and have fun.

Naveen's valet, Lawrence, wasn't so happy-go-lucky, but then poor Lawrence had to carry all the cases!

Tiana was far too busy to pay attention to the prince. But she was delighted when Charlotte came to call with her rich father, "Big Daddy" LaBouff.

"Did you hear?" bubbled Charlotte. "Big Daddy invited Prince Naveen to our masquerade ball tonight!" Beaming, she added, "I'm going to need about 500 of your man-catching beignets."

PRINCE ARRIVES TODAY

Naveen

CHE
50 I
W

To Be Held

Prince Naveen of Maldonia
WORLDS MOST
ELIGIBLE BACHELOR

Charlotte's payment for the beignets meant that Tiana finally had enough money to make an offer for the old sugar mill and turn it into her dream restaurant. She met the owners, the Fenner brothers, and struck a deal.

"Table for one, please!" called a voice behind Tiana. It was her mother, with a very special present – her father's old gumbo pot!

Meanwhile, in the French Quarter, Naveen and Lawrence had been lured into the lair of a strange man called Dr. Facilier. He promised that he could give them everything their hearts desired – but Facilier was a sorcerer, and he had an evil plan in mind. The room came alive with bad magic, and the spell was cast!

At the mansion, Prince Naveen made a grand
entrance to the masquerade. Tiana had delivered
her beignets and was dressed up for the party –
but then she met the Fenner brothers. They had
bad news – the sugar mill deal was off!

"Fella came in offering the full amount in cash,"
said one of the brothers. "Unless you can top his
offer by Wednesday..."

Tiana was crushed. As she reached out to plead
with them, Tiana
toppled into her own
beignet stand and
ruined her dress!

Charlotte was very kind. She took Tiana up to her room and loaned her a beautiful gown, worthy of a princess.

Tiana stood on the balcony and looked at the twinkling Evening Star. "I cannot believe I'm doing this," she said as she made a wish that she would get her restaurant. When she was finished, she opened her eyes and saw... a frog!

"I suppose you want me to kiss you?" said Tiana.

"Kissing would be nice, yes!" said the frog.

Tiana shrieked and ran back into the room.

"Please allow me to introduce myself," begged the frog. "I am Prince Naveen of Maldonia!"

But if the frog was Prince Naveen... who was that dancing with Charlotte?

Naveen explained that Tiana's kiss would transform him back into a human. "Surely I could offer you some type of reward!" he begged.

Tiana felt sorry for the little frog. Plus she really did want her restaurant. And though it went against all her beliefs, she leaned in, closed her eyes – and kissed him. POOF!

"Aaiieeeeee!" screamed Tiana. The magic had gone wrong. The frog had not turned into a prince. Instead, the princess had turned into a frog!

It didn't happen like that in the stories. But then, Tiana wasn't really a princess – she had just been dressed up as one.

Frantic, the two frogs jumped out of the window.

Meanwhile, the "prince" confessed to Dr. Facilier that he had accidentally let the frog escape! The doctor had used his magic to change Prince Naveen into a frog – and make Lawrence look like Naveen! He wanted Charlotte to marry the fake prince, so that he could get his hands on Big Daddy's money. But Facilier needed the frog to refill the talisman around Lawrence's neck, to keep him looking like Naveen.

By now, Tiana and Naveen had reached the bayou. They made a raft and Tiana steered it while lazy Naveen took it easy. But then a huge alligator popped up from the water! Luckily, the alligator just wanted to talk about jazz music. His name was Louis and he had a beautiful trumpet called Giselle.

Tiana explained that she and Naveen weren't really frogs – they were under a spell. Louis knew someone who could help them.

"Mama Odie. She's got magic!" he said.

On the way to Mama Odie's home, they met a firefly called Ray, with a glowing tail, and had a brush with a trio of ruthless frog hunters. Naveen bravely helped Tiana escape their clutches, and Tiana began to realise that Naveen had some good qualities after all.

As they floated downriver, the four friends looked up at the night sky.

"There's Evangeline," said Ray. "She is the prettiest firefly that ever did glow." But Tiana knew that Ray was really looking at the Evening Star.

Louis played his trumpet softly, while Tiana and Naveen danced on a lily pad. What a perfect, romantic evening...

Dr. Facilier sent dark shadow spirits to find Naveen, but they arrived at Mama Odie's house too late. FOOM! Mama Odie cast a dazzling spell and drove the shadows away.

"Not bad for a 197-year-old blind lady!" she said.

Her home was an old shrimp boat, nestling in a tree, and she had a pet snake called JuJu. Mama Odie knew why the frogs had come – they wanted her to make them human again.

Mama Odie conjured an image in a tub of gumbo. It showed Charlotte and her father. Big Daddy was to be king of Mardi Gras, and that would make Charlotte a princess. If Naveen kissed Charlotte – a princess until midnight – he and Tiana would both be human again.

The friends jumped on a riverboat and chugged back to New Orleans. Naveen confessed to Ray that he had fallen in love with Tiana.

But before he could declare his love to Tiana, she excitedly pointed out the sugar mill.

Suddenly, Naveen realised that he did not have enough money to help Tiana get what she wanted the most. He would never be able to help buy the sugar mill by tomorrow's deadline. Sadly, Naveen walked away...

But poor Naveen didn't get far! He was captured by the shadow spirits and taken to Dr. Facilier.

"Ah, much obliged, Gentlemen," said Facilier to the shadows.

With the magic refilled in the talisman, Lawrence turned back into the handsome prince.

Facilier locked Naveen inside a small chest and carried him off.

The fake prince soon won Charlotte's heart. Their wedding was to be part of the Mardi Gras parade. Ray and Tiana raced back to watch.

Tiana didn't realise that this prince was Lawrence in disguise. She couldn't understand how her beloved Naveen could marry someone else.

But Ray knew that Naveen would never do that.
He went searching for his friend and found him
locked in the chest. Ray soon set Naveen free.

Just as the bogus prince was about to say "I do",
Naveen grabbed the magic charm from around
his neck and tossed it to Ray, who flew off with it.
Facilier chased after him while Lawrence turned
back into himself and stayed hidden.

At the cemetery, Ray tossed the talisman to Tiana, just before Facilier knocked him to the ground and stepped on him.

Facilier tried to persuade Tiana to give him the charm. But Tiana remembered what her daddy had told her about never losing sight of what is important. She threw it to the ground, smashing it.

The shadows turned on Facilier and soon, all that was left of him was his top hat.

Naveen found Charlotte and explained everything to her. If she kissed him before midnight, he and Tiana would become human. Then he would marry Charlotte, if she would give Tiana the money to buy the sugar mill.

"Wait!" Tiana shouted. Naveen turned to her in surprise. "My dream wouldn't be complete without you in it."

Realising her friend was in love, Charlotte looked at Naveen. "I'll kiss you, Your Highness. No marriage required!" But her kiss was too late. The clock struck midnight!

Charlotte was no longer Mardi Gras princess. They had missed their chance!

Tiana and Naveen were still frogs, but they had found true love. Sadly, their joy was interrupted when Louis appeared, carrying a leaf with an injured Ray on it.

Naveen told Ray, "We're staying together."

"I like that very much," Ray said. "Evangeline likes that, too." Then his little light flickered out for the last time.

When Ray's friends looked up, there was a new star next to the Evening Star.

Ray had been right. True love always finds a way.

In the morning, Tiana and Naveen got married.
As Naveen kissed his new wife, he and Tiana
turned back into humans!

"Once you became my wife, that made you... "
Naveen began.

"A princess," Tiana finished. "You just kissed a
princess!"

Later, Tiana and
Naveen got married
again, this time with all
their friends and family
in attendance.

But the new royal couple didn't become lazy. They did buy their restaurant, and the food was the best anyone had ever tasted. The music, thanks to Louis, was swinging. Everyone agreed that Tiana's Palace was special.

Finally, Tiana had everything she had ever dreamed of.